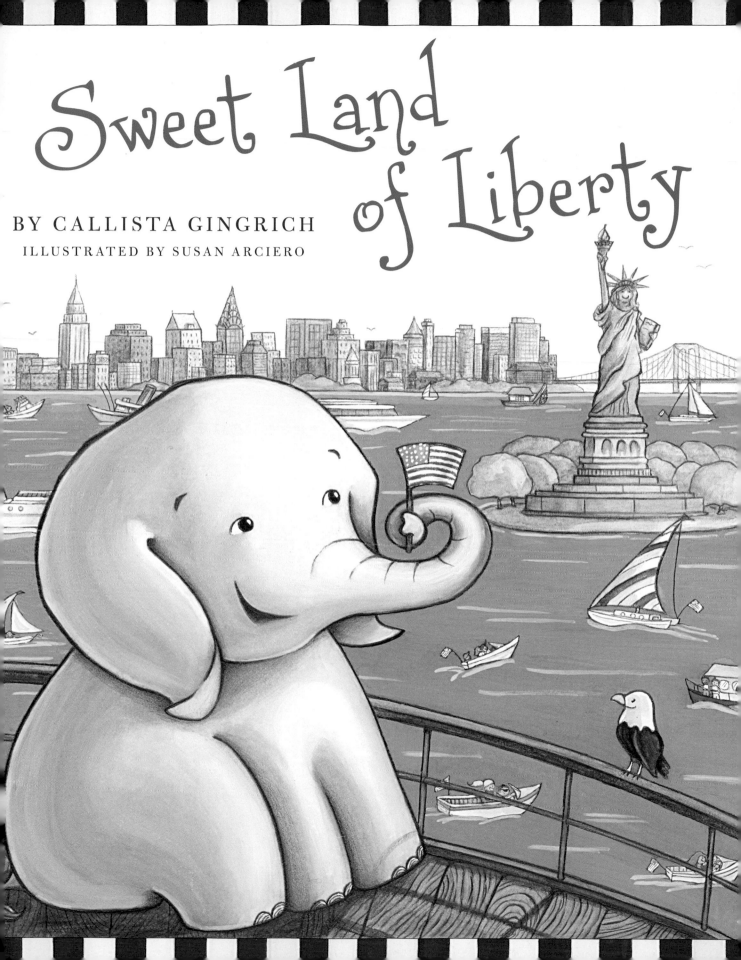

Sweet Land of Liberty

BY CALLISTA GINGRICH

ILLUSTRATED BY SUSAN ARCIERO

★ ★ ★ ★ ★ Acknowledgments ★ ★ ★ ★ ★

Thank you to the remarkable group of dedicated people who made this book possible.

I especially want to thank the talented Susan Arciero, whose illustrations have brought Ellis the Elephant to life.

The team at Regnery Publishing has made writing and publishing *Sweet Land of Liberty* a real joy. Special thanks to Marji Ross, Jeff Carneal, Amanda Larsen, Kathleen Sweetapple, and Eleanor Reed for their insightful and creative contributions. Regnery has been remarkable in turning this book into a reality.

My deepest gratitude goes to our staff, including, Michelle Selesky, Christina Maruna, Alicia Melvin, Anna Haberlein, Bess Kelly, Ross Worthington, Caitlin Laverdiere, Vince Haley, and Kathy Lubbers whose assistance in this project has been invaluable.

Finally, I'd like to thank my husband, Newt. His enthusiasm for Ellis the Elephant and *Sweet Land of Liberty* has been my true inspiration.

Library of Congress Cataloging-in-Publication Data

Gingrich, Callista.
Sweet land of liberty / by Callista Gingrich; illustrated by Susan Arciero.
p. cm.
ISBN 978-1-59698-292-5
1. United States--History--Juvenile literature. I. Arciero, Susan,
ill. II. Title.
E178.3.G534 2011
973--dc23
2011032964

Published in the United States by
Regnery Publishing, Inc.
One Massachusetts Avenue, NW
Washington, DC 20001
www.regnery.com

Manufactured in the United States of America

10 9 8 7 6 5 4

Books are available in quantity for promotional or premium use.
For information on discounts and terms write to Director of Special Sales, Regnery Publishing, Inc.,
One Massachusetts Avenue, NW, Washington, DC, 20001, or call 202-216-0600.

Distributed to the trade by:
Perseus Distribution
387 Park Avenue South
New York, NY 10016

To American Patriots, young and old,
who make America a special nation.

★ ★ ★ ★ ★

Ellis the Elephant was a smart little guy,
with a curly grey trunk, and a twinkling eye.
He liked asking questions, he was eager to see
how America became the land of the free!

Ellis went to the library, an amazing place,
and looked at the books with a grin on his face.
"These books hold the secret, I'm sure it is true,
why America is special, full of red, white, and blue."

In his first book he read how America began.
Brave pilgrims came here to find a new land.
With the help of God, they survived cold and beast,
and celebrated together with a Thanksgiving feast.

As the years went on, more and more settlers came.
They formed thirteen colonies, none quite the same.
But on one sure thing they would all agree:
The King would not rule them — they would be free.

But the King didn't listen, and passed a tax on tea.
The colonists said, "We won't pay a fee!"
They jumped on the ships and caused a real commotion.
Then they threw the English tea right into the ocean.

"All men are created equal," the people did say.
"We have rights from God that can't be taken away."
Together in Philadelphia, our Founding Fathers in attendance,
the colonies declared, "We must have independence!"

That independence was not so easily won.
It would take years of fighting and fighting's not fun.
But there was a great man who helped lead the way.
George Washington, the Father of our Country, we say.

Across the Delaware he led the troops in freezing rain and snow.
Throughout the Revolution much bravery did he show!
After winning the war, Washington would not become a king.
He became our first president, and that's a better thing.

Ellis found another book, with more presidents reflected,
all chosen by the people, every one of them elected!
Abraham Lincoln was a president who did a lot of reading
to be well prepared for the country he'd be leading.

Ellis learned that Lincoln was called "Honest Abe,"
he became a great hero for freeing the slaves.
Throughout the Civil War, President Lincoln stood tall.
His leadership was admired by one and by all.

Ellis read of cowboys going west across the plains,
as families rode together in covered wagon trains.

This long journey would put their courage to the test,
but the settlers didn't stop and forward on they pressed.
These Americans were known as the great pioneers,
and they would learn to prosper on the new frontier.

Ellis learned that in America we are free to live our dreams.
With much work we do great things, as hard as they may seem!
Thomas Edison made the light bulb, Alexander Graham Bell the phone.
When the Wright Brothers invented the airplane,
it was the first time anyone had flown!

Ellis read of those coming from distant shores,
arriving in a country they had never seen before.
Speaking different languages, they all shared a dream —
to live together in a land where freedom was supreme.

There were so many people coming to this spot,
that America became known as "the great melting pot!"
Through Ellis Island these new Americans came.
And Ellis was delighted, just to read his name!

Ellis read on about generations past.
He learned what they did to make freedom last.

Our freedom was earned by great women and men.
We must never forget how brave they have been.
They boldly stood up when their country did call.
Without them we might not have freedom at all!

Ellis learned of the race to put a man on the moon.
President Kennedy said, "We must do it soon!"

Many watched as the rocket flew into the sky.
Bound for the moon, the astronauts did fly.
They raised a flag and began to explore.
It was something that no one had done before.

As the afternoon passed, Ellis read of the deeds,
that many have done to help those in need.

Whenever there's a challenge, be it far or near,
Americans are more than ready to volunteer.

Ellis packed up his trunk, he was done for the day.
He would come back tomorrow and keep reading away.

Now it was time for a celebration —
a birthday party for our great nation.
Ellis watched the fireworks and could clearly see,
that America is special — the land of the free!

★ ★ ★ ★ ★ Resources ★ ★ ★ ★ ★

Fun Places to Learn More about Exceptional Moments in American History

Air and Space Museum

This is an exciting museum for anyone interested in planes, space, astronauts, military, or science. There are two museums that house many planes, space suits, and even a space ship.

Admission is free, and tours are also free. Ticket purchases are required to see the IMAX movies. ★ There are two Smithsonian Air and Space Museums in Washington, DC: Independence Avenue at 6th Street, SW, Washington, DC and 14390 Air and Space Museum Parkway, Chantilly, VA 20151 ★ For more information on planning your visit, go to http://www.nasm.si.edu/ ★ Call for general information at: 202-633-1000.

Boston Tea Party Ships & Museum

Three restored and recreated ships, the *Beaver*, the *Dartmouth*, and the *Eleanor* are located in the Boston harbor, and visitors can go on board. The neighboring museum houses exhibits on colonial life and the events that led to the Boston Tea Party and the American Revolution.

Location: Congress Street Bridge, Boston, MA 02127 ★ For more information, visit http://www.bostonteapartyship.com/ ★ Call for general information at: (617) 737-3317.

Colonial Williamsburg

Colonial Williamsburg is the largest living history museum in the world with 301 acres depicting what life was like in colonial, pre-revolutionary times. Go inside the restored buildings, talk to the many costumed historical interpreters, and you will feel as if you have traveled back in time.

Location: Williamsburg, VA ★ You must purchase tickets to go to Colonial Williamsburg, and there are

many different ticket options that you can find on the website. There are so many things to do here that you may want to plan a two- or three-day visit. ★ For information on planning your visit, go to www.colonialwilliamsburg.com ★ Call for general information at: 757-229-1000.

Ellis Island

The Ellis Island Immigration Museum became part of the Statue of Liberty National Monument by presidential proclamation in 1965, and it is one of the country's most popular historic sites. In addition to stories about the 12 million immigrants who entered America here, you will find the American Family Immigration History Center®, which provides visitors with technology, printed materials, and professional assistance for investigating immigration history, family documentation, and genealogical exploration.

Location: Liberty Island, New York, NY 10004-1467. ★ Access to the Ellis Island Immigration Museum and the grounds surrounding the main building is free. ★ Ferry tickets can be obtained ONLY from the Statue Cruises ferry company, in one of three ways: 1) Call 1-877-LADY-TIX (1-877-523-9849), 2) On-line at: www.statuecruises.com, or 3) Same day at the ferry ticket box office in Castle Clinton in Battery Park, New York City, or at Liberty State Park in New Jersey. ★ Call for general information at: 212-363-3200.

Historic National Red Cross Headquarters

This building, which was declared a National Historic Landmark in 1965, houses art and artifacts acquired by the American Red Cross since it was created in 1881.

Location: 430 17th Street, Washington, DC 20006 ★ For more information, go to: http://www.redcross.org/museum/history/visitorinfo.asp ★ Call for general information at: 202-303-7066.

★ ★ ★ ★ ★ Resources ★ ★ ★ ★ ★

Fun Places to Learn More about Exceptional Moments in American History

Independence Hall, Philadelphia

Independence Hall is where America's founding fathers came together to discuss declaring American independence from Great Britain. In 1776, they signed the Declaration of Independence here, and after the Revolutionary War, they came back to Independence Hall to create one of the most important documents ever written: The Constitution. When you visit, you can go inside Independence Hall to see where these historic events took place, and you can walk across the street to see the Liberty Bell or the Constitution Center.

Location: Independence Visitor Center, 525 Market Street, Philadelphia, PA ★ It is best to park at the Independence Visitor Center's underground parking garage, located on the east (left) side of 6th Street between Arch and Market Streets. ★ Tickets are required to go inside Independence Hall. For tickets call 1-877-444-6777 or visit www.recreation.gov ★ For more information on planning your visit, go to http://www.nps.gov/inde/planyourvisit/index.htm ★ Call for general information at: 215-965-2305

Iwo Jima Memorial

Iwo Jima, Japan was the site of a very severe World War II battle, which became immortalized with a photograph taken of Marines raising the American flag above the destruction of the battle. A life-sized statue honoring the United States Marines and depicting this moment can be seen at the Iwo Jima Memorial in Arlington, VA.

Location: Marshall Drive, Arlington, VA ★ This memorial is free and open daily, but you may want to visit when the Marine Corps presents the Marine Sunset Review Parade on Tuesdays from 7:00 to 8:30 PM, May through August.

Kennedy Space Center

This is the location where space ships blast off. When you visit, you can get behind-the-scenes tours of the space center, take a ride in the flight simulator, and feel as if you are witnessing the Apollo moon program first-hand.

Location: SR 405, Kennedy Space Center, FL ★ The admission price is $43 for adults/$33 for children (ages 3-11), plus tax. Kennedy Space Center admission includes IMAX® space movies, all exhibits and shows, plus the U.S. Astronaut Hall of Fame® and interactive space-flight simulators. ★ For more information on planning your visit, go to http://www.kennedyspacecenter.com/ ★ Call for general information at: 321-449-4444.

Laura Ingalls Wilder Historic Home and Museum

(author of *Little House on the Prairie*)

The museum exhibits include artifacts that span over a century of the pioneering history described in Laura Ingalls Wilder's famous "Little House on the Prairie" books.

Location: 3068 Highway A, Mansfield, MO 65704 ★ For more information, visit http://www.lauraingallswilderhome.com ★ Call for general information at: 417-924-3626.

Library of Congress

This is the official library for the United States Congress. Built in 1800, the Library of Congress is the largest library in the world. Anyone can visit, but only congressmen, Supreme Court justices, and other important elected officials are able to check out books.

Location: 10 First Street, SE, Washington, DC ★ The closest public transportation Metro stop is Capitol South on the Orange line. The library is across the street from the Capitol and next door to the Supreme Court. ★ There is no charge to visit the Library of Congress , and free tours are offered. Visit http://www.loc.gov/index.html for more information. ★ Call for general information at: 202- 707-9779.

★ ★ ★ ★ ★ Resources ★ ★ ★ ★ ★

Fun Places to Learn More about Exceptional Moments in American History

Lincoln Memorial

The Lincoln Memorial was built to honor President Abraham Lincoln. This is also the site where Dr. Martin Luther King gave his famous "I Have a Dream" speech 100 years after President Lincoln issued the Emancipation Proclamation, freeing slaves in America. The Lincoln Memorial is pictured on the back of the five dollar bill and on the back of the penny.

Location: The National Mall, Washington, DC ★ Visits to the Lincoln Memorial are free, and you can also go to the surrounding free Smithsonian museums. Visit the website at http://www.nps.gov/linc/index.htm ★ Call for general information at: 202-426-6841.

Plymouth Rock

Plymouth Rock lies on the original site where the first pilgrims landed their boat in America in 1620. Visiting Plymouth Rock, you can not only see the rock, but you can also visit many interesting and historical museums. You can even visit a colonial plantation.

Location: Visitor's Center, 130 Water Street, Plymouth, MA ★ For information about all activities in Plymouth, visit www.visit-plymouth.com ★ Call for general information at: 508-747-7525.

Statue of Liberty

This symbol of freedom was given to the United States by France in 1886. Lady Liberty holds a torch of freedom with her right hand and a book of law in her left, enlightening the world with America's freedom and democracy.

Location: Liberty Island, New York, NY 10004-1467 ★ You can take a Ferry to Liberty Island from Battery Park and Liberty State Park. Visit www.statuecruises.com to buy Ferry Tickets. ★ There is no cost to visit Liberty Island, but in order to go inside the Statue of Liberty, you must make reservations in advance:

http://www.nps.gov/stli/planyourvisit/feesandreservations.htm ★ Call for general information at: 212 363-3200.

Valley Forge

Valley Forge is where George Washington and his troops spent the harsh winter of 1777 during the Revolutionary War. When you visit, you can have a guided tour of the park and see historical reenactments on special dates.

Location: Valley Forge, PA ★ There is no entrance fee but Trolley Tour and Step-on Tour reservations may be made through The Encampment Store at 610-783-1074. ★ For more information on planning your visit, go to http://www.nps.gov/vafo/index.htm ★ Call for general information at: 610-783-1077.

World War II Memorial

This monument honors those who fought in World War II. Located near the Lincoln Memorial and the Washington Monument, this is one of the newer memorials, built in 2004. When you visit, be sure to find your home state, as the memorial pays tribute to all 50 states.

Location: 17th Street, between Constitution and Independence Avenues, Washington, DC. ★ For more information on planning your visit, go to www.nps.gov/nwwm ★ Call for general information at: 202-619-7222.

Wright Brothers National Memorial

Kitty Hawk, North Carolina is where the Wright Brothers flew the first airplane. When you visit, you can see replicas of their aircrafts, including a full scale replica of their 1903 Flying Machine. You can also stand on the actual spot where the first flight took place.

Location: Highway 158, Kill Devil Hills, NC ★ Ages 15 and under are admitted free, and for those aged 16 and up, admission is $4. For more information, visit the website at http://www.nps.gov/wrbr/index.htm ★ Call for general information at: 252-473-2111.